SUBLIME LOVE

Flairs and Glairs
Publication House

"Sublime Love"

ISBN No: " 978-93-91302-60-3"
1st Edition
Language – English and Hindi

Flairs and Glairs
Publication House
Regd. Under MSME Act.

Disclaimer

This is a work of fiction and solely represent the thoughts of the corresponding authors of the articles. Our editors have tried their best to edit the content of all the authors and check the plagiarism.

All the write-ups in this book are unique and are only published in this book.

In case any plagiarism or error is found, only the author is responsible alone, and not the publisher or the Compilers.

Cover Designing and Book Formatting
Shubham Shah and Ishani Agarwal

Acknowledgement

The completion of this undertaking could not have been possible without the participation and assistance of so many people whose names may not all be enumerated. Gratitude towards all the co-authors, those have toiled hard to make this book to be successful one.

We are thankful to Flairs And Glairs publication, without whom, this project would never have been possible. Moreover heartfelt thanks to our parents, family, relatives and friends for their continuous support and encouragement towards us in completing this book. Above all to the Great, Almighty, the author of knowledge and wisdom, for his countless love.

Co-Authors

Shubham Shah (Founder Flairs and Glairs)
Ishani Agarwal (Co-Founder Flairs and Glairs)
Lipsa Sahoo (Compiler)

1) Sanjay Naik
2) Swasti Smaranika Sahoo
3) Priya Singh
4) Krutika Satish Ghanekar
5) T. Poojalakshmi
6) Arsh Abid
7) Kajal Bhavsar Bhatt
8) Trupti Prabha Sahu
9) B. Anamika
10) Ashis Pahi
11) Deepanshu Arora
12) Saloni Kumari
13) Krishan Kant Sen
14) Mansha Poddar
15) Sumit Naseem
16) V. Rathika
17) Pragya Verma
18) Jeevitha. S
19) Aishwarya V.J
20) Nomita Baidya
21) Anupama Baidya
22) Aman Sharma
23) Konki Kamal Sharon
24) Rubleena Behera
25) Updesh Carpenter
26) Ashish Kumar Pathak
27) Riya Vishnoi
28) Monalisha Panda

29) Krishna Kanthi Tilak G
30) Aniruddha Deepak Gohil
31) Debapriyo Rout
32) Meenakshi
33) Shivanjali Srivastava
34) Mahitixa Tank
35) Shivangi Srivastava
36) Jhunu Swain
37) Romy Kumar
38) Ajay Borasi
39) Zainab Saboowala
40) Anwesha Maharana
41) Rachna Sandip Mistry
42) Ankita Deb
43) Yamini Manchineni
44) Sitara Akula
45) Manoj Sondhiya
46) Prasad Babu Galla
47) Sanjeet Kumar
48) Naina Deka
49) Aman Agarwal
50) Puja Bagarti
51) Rajesh Kumar Sahoo
52) Sandhiya. S
53) Showmen Talukdar
54) Sparsh Kulshretha

Shubham Shah

(Founder- Flairs and Glairs)

Shubham Shah, an entrepreneur at "Flairs & Glairs" a brand with dynamics in events organizing and cultural educational pan INDIA, is a 26yrs old guy who recently has entered the digital platform of imprinting emotions. He has initiated with his own open mic platform to help budding poets and aspiring writers under his brand named as "Teekhe Zasbaaat"

He is a commerce graduate from the Bhagalpur City of Bihar.

He states Writing has impersonated him since childhood and he has now been writing for over a decade!

Cooking, on the other hand, is his passion! He also mentions, trying out new things just tickles him!

When asked sir, Why SPICY EMOTIONS?

He smiled and added, "agar jasbaat teekhe na ho toh wo jasbaat kahan" Spices are all that blends! So do his words!

As a chef, he presents to you his dish! Hot and freshly served! Taste it! Feel it! Enjoy it! You can also find his writing in the Book "Teekhe Zasbaaat" and 50+ Co-authored anthologies. With his passion to explore opportunities across Platforms, he is working with keen devotion and We wish him all the very best for his future ventures.

He is Featured in the International Magazine DeMode for his upcoming solo novel.

He is Approved by Ne8x for its Lit Fest, and is a Golden Star Awards 2020 Winner.

He is a India Book of Records Holder for his Anthology Satrang, and has the Grandmaster title by Asia Book of Records, for the same.

He has also been featured in Prabhat Khabar, Dainik Jagran, and a lot of other Newspapers in Bihar for his achievements.

He has been a proud co-author to

India Book Of Records (Title- Black)

World Book Of Records (Title -15 Wonders of Poetries)

India Book Of Records (Title - Aaina)

Vajra World Records Holder (Title - Gustakhi Maaf Hai)

High Range of Records Holder (Title - Gustakhi Maaf Hai)

Indian Book of Records

(Title - Road from Worst to Best)

Share your reviews on his

INSTAGRAM

@spicy_emotions
@shubham4shah

Or via email on

shubham2shah@gmail.com

To stay tuned to his work and opportunities follow his business Handles

INSTAGRAM   FACEBOOK   YOUTUBE

@flairsandglairs
@teekhezasbaaat

WEBSITE:

https://flairsandglairs.in/
https://flairsandglairs.com/

Ishani Agarwal

(Co-Founder- Flairs and Glairs)

Ishani Agarwal hails from the City of Joy, Kolkata.

She is the co-founder of her Community "Teekhe Zasbaaat" and Flairs and Glairs Publication.

Been a Compiler for 45+ Anthologies, she is in the process for more. Co-authored in 150+ Anthologies. She is a India Book of Records Holder, a Vajra World Records Holder, a High Range of Records Holder, an OMG Book of Records Holder, a Bravo Record holder, a Forever Star Book of World Records and an Indian Book of Records Holder.

Approved by Ne8x for its Lit Fest 2020, and Literary Icon 2020. Also a Golden Star Awards Winner 2020.

She has also been awarded with India Star Republic Award 2021, a part of She Awards by Awards Arc and Winner of Nari Samman 2021 by Literoma.

She is also selected as Best Achiever of the Year by AwardsArc and Most Challenging Compiler Award by Spectrum Awards.
She got her first solo Published,a solo Compilation consisting of first 750 contents of hers, titled "Hand That Burnt While Healing".

She has been featured by the National Magazine "Taree Zameen Par" with the title 'unstoppable'.
Also featured in the International Magazine DeMode for her upcoming solo novel, she is proud to write on social issues, and is happy with the love she is receiving.
Connect with her on Instagram: @Ishani_agarwal_quotes / @compilations_so_far

COMPILER
LIPSA SAHOO

She is Lipsa Sahoo, from Jajpur, Odisha. She is nineteen years old. Currently she is pursuing her graduation in English honors at Vyasanagar Autonomous College, Jajpur Road, Odisha. She started her writing career, just after the completion of her 12th Board examination. Writing is her passion and she aims to come across millions of hearts through this. Heartfelt thanks to her beloved father, for his continuous love, care and support towards her.

Instagram Handle: lipsa_sahoo.01

Love

Love is the most precious and pleasurable feeling in the world. It is the divine power, which can challenge even the most dreadful disease in the world. Love is the amazing sentiment, which can't be defined using the twenty six English alphabets.

True and pure love is very hard to find. True love is something, which is just the opposite of materialistic pleasure. True love is the union of two souls. Though the bodies of true lovers can be separated, their souls can never be separated. Distance doesn't matter for true lovers because they are internally connected.

Genuine love is something, which happens once in a lifetime and stays immortal. One's first love is true one, free from all kinds of materialistic glee.

मेरे पापा

जब से होश संभाला मैंने उस
बचपन में लेकर चल दो ना
उंगली पकड़कर साथ मेरा दो
चार कदम आगे चल दो ना
चलते-चलते थक जाऊं तो गोद
में अपनी भर लो ना
'रानी' बेटा कहकर मुझको फिर
सुनने का वो हक दो ना।

चेहरा मेरा तुम पढ़कर कुछ
बातें ख़ुद समझ लो ना
और कहने से पहले आंखों
से राज़ पकड़ लो ना
रोते-रोते घुट जाऊं तो सर
पर हाथ संवर दो ना
फिर जब हिम्मत हारूं तो
कसकर सीने से तुम जकड़
लो ना।

जीवन के हर पहलू को अपने
अनुभव से बता दो ना
और जो बारिश दुख के बरसे
उस गुत्थी को सुलझा दो ना
बाबा मेरे पास बैठकर यादो
को एक पहर दो ना
आंखें मेरी भीगी तो पल-पल
मुस्कान ऐसी भर दो ना।

SWASTI SMARANIKA SAHOO

The Platonic Love For You

From the beginning of civilization, love is always there for. But in the course of time the purity of love has changed;not in all form only besides some relations which will never change anyway. No need to explain those as we have idea about it.

The fact is that I can't express my feelings for you as the perspective of the society has madly unveiled. I want to spend times with you, share my talks with you, make mini programmes with you. But my bad that I only can dream that before alliance. The naked mentality of the society accepts the molestation of a kid but can't see the spiritual love in a right manner. I've something for you beyond the reality, above the materialistic love but a pure soul, a spirit searching heart that only feels for you. The society may bark by identifying us together or may be envious by observing our love. May our fate won't support us, still I'm madly love with you. Your slight attention is my happiest property. Your smile is my pain killer and you are my everlasting love. I don't need life to be with you but I need you to be alive. Some says heart stoling is love but I say two hearts & one life is love. Love has a plenty definition. Not a single line or a rack of books can define that but the deeper you explore love the brighter it blossoms apart.

PRIYA SINGH

Sublime-"Everlasting love, Two hearts one life."

Love is not only a feeling,
it's an emotion as sea,
Once you dipped into
it, you couldn't fly away
from it. Two hearts together,
as one life, they come along
together or none. Feeling always
remain same whether other one
physically stands or not.
-

Love is like a Rose.
It's every petals so close,
when you smell it,
it enthralls,
spellbound by it's charm
whoever gets so close.
-

A few more lines beautifully depicted the theme.
*Love is a butterfly,
It has many different colors
& wings to fly,
It seems so light & every moment modify.
It drifts people in deep, could anyone think of why????
Love is a butterfly,
you could see it a moment, you wish to grab it another one,
It either close up people or blows them away.
people go insanely crazy, could anyone think of it why???
Love is a butterfly,
It either simplifies all
or messes up everything ally.

Even sane people have gone insanely crazy, could anyone think of it. Why???
Love is a butterfly,
It seems all good until another one
bothers to try, to put efforts in it.
It seems deliberate but it's not.
people get bounded together either in love
or in envy. Could anyone think of it & tell me why???

# KRUTIKA SATISH GHANEKAR

Love - An Immortal Bond

Love is an art,
Spreads from our heart,
Meant to attach and never makes apart.

Signifies affection and care,
Makes a lovely pair,
But lasts only if it's true & fair !

T.POOJALAKSHMI

Quotes On "You And Me"

1. The thought of being with you makes me happy. When I am with you, even the impossible things become possible to me....

2. Let's drown in our everlasting love to become one heart and one soul...

3. It's not matters how we begin our love... It's matters how we journey in our love life...

4. Everytime when I dream of you, a smile comes over my lips automatically....

5. If I were the music, then you would be my string of love....

6. I wish to walk in your path which has become true but later I discovered that I have become your path.....

7. I can sense your presence even when you are away from me...

8. When you hold me in your arms, I can feel your warmth and love for me....

9. When two hearts are connected, even their thoughts and actions are also be connected if we keenly observe it...

10. When I say " I Love You" to you, it's not from my lips dear... It's purely from the bottom of my heart love....

ARSH ABID

इन बदलती फ़िज़ाओं से मुतस्सिर ना होना,
ऐ इश्क़ करने वालों महबूब क़रीब तो आया है तुम्हारे,
मगर दिल तोड़ने के लिए तुम इसे इश्क़ ना समझ बेठना।

KAJAL BHAVSAR BHATT

No, I don't miss you anymore

No, I don't miss you anymore;
Although we had great moments together

You left me saying you don't trust me;
Don't you think it was enough for me?

We talked a lot, laughed and cried together;
When I shared my feelings, you made fun of my call

It hurt me a lot, I changed my number; to make a healthy
distance and remove you from my world

Now you have come to ask,
If I am married or not

My feelings were just fun?
Were we passing time for the lust?

I've become different currently
I've got goals and ambitions widely

I can't be with anybody,
I am changed completely,
Which I've learnt from you only

TRUPTI PRABHA SAHU

Let Go Of Your Stresses!

A physiologist walked around a room while teaching stress management to an audience. As she raised a glass of water, everyone expected they'd be asked the "half empty or half full" question. Instead with a smile on her face, she inquired:"How heavy is this glass of water? "

Answers called out ranged from 8 oz. to 20 oz.
She replied,"The absolute weight doesn't matter. It depends on how long I hold it. If I hold it for a minute, it's not a problem. I hold it for an hour, I'll have an ache in my arm. If I hold it for a day, my arm will feel numb and paralysed. In each case the weight of the glass doesn't change, but the longer I hold it, it heavier it becomes. "

She continued," The stresses and worries in my life are like that glass of water. Think about them for a while and nothing happens. Think about them a bit longer and they begin to hurt. And if you think about them all day long, you'll feel paralysed--incapable of doing anything. "

-It's important to remember to let go of your Stresses. As early in the evening as you can, put all your burdens down. Don't carry them through the evening and into the night Remember to put the glass down!

B.ANAMIKA

Two Souls One Density

The best thing in life is unseen that is the heart and a soul. When two souls fall in love there is nothing else to be happen. Loving someone was never something which have to be planned it just happened.

When you loved someone and too and too late to be the first. Then you have to prepare yourself to be the everlast.

The love is true density the path to love is our spiritual density. Love bears all things and believes all things and that love never ends.

Every relations has two hearts and two souls but a single thought. Love is composed of a single soul inhabiting two bodies. It's spiritual.

When you know you are in Love you can't fall asleep. Living with a loved one's feels like everything we have. Be kind what you loved you must Love. With the entirety of your inner souls.

Understanding:

Love means what? According to me, Its an emotionally attached bonding of two body and mind. There is no impact and importance of soul in love. Soul and heart are far different from love and its an illusionary thought.
Have you ever seen the bonding of our parents? If Yes, then it's the real and true love. Before 30-40 years ago parents don't even know who will be there life partner and how they will survive with an unknown person. But after marriage there bonding start to begin and a new journey starts for both of the couples. Day by day they comes closer to each other and their love didn't sink rather it becomes more stronger than previous day. Todays love is a biased form of love and affection.

DEEPANSHU ARORA

चाँद सी मोहब्बत

तुम्हारी मोहब्बत भी चाँद की तरह है......
नूर भी उतना ही....
गुरुर भी उतना ही.......
और मुझसे दूर भी उतना ही!!!!

सच मे तुम्हारा इश्क़ चांद की ही तरह है.......
ठंडक भी उसके जैसी
चांदनी भी कुछ कुछ वैसी
और तो और उसमें बेवफाई भी है
मानो चांद में लगे दाग जैसी

पलके झुका कर बैठा हूँ मैं....
पलके झुका कर बैठा हूँ मैं.....
तुझे देख लेने के इंतज़ार में......
पर तेरा दीदार भी कुछ ऐसा हुआ जैसे ....
ग्रहण लगा हो उसी चाँद में!!!

मज़हब से तेरे कभी वाकिफ ना हो पाया......
मज़हब से तेरे कभी वाकिफ ना हो पाया.....
क्यूंकि तेरा मज़बह भी उस चाँद की तरह निकला.....
जो कभी ईद का तो कभी करवाचौथ का नज़र आया!!!

इंतेज़ार तेरा फिर भी हर शाम के बाद रहता है......
इंतेज़ार तेरा फिर भी हर शाम के बाद रहता है......
क्यूँकि जानता हूँ कि हर डूबते सूरज के साथ......
चाँद निकल कर जरूर आता हैं!!!!

SALONI KUMARI

जिंदगी

जिंदगी के हर मोड़ पर
इक सवाल दिल में आता है
जिंदगी का वो खुशनुमा पल
क्यों नहीं ठहर जाता है

दिवाने हम भी हो गये थे
पर दिवानगी कहा समझ आता है
ये तो दरिया है
समुंदर में मिलते ही
न जाने कहाँ खो जाता है

ये जो जिंदगी का उलझन है
हर किसी को कहा समझ आता है
जो समझ जाता है
वो सम्भल जाता है

हर किसी के जिंदगी में   कुछ अच्छा तो कुछ बुरा वक्त आता है
इन हालातों में कोई जिंदगी खो देता है
तो कोई जीना सीख जाता है
जिंदगी के हर मोड़ पर
इक सवाल दिल में आता है
जिंदगी का वो खुशनुमा पल
क्यों नहीं ठहर जाता है

प्यार न सही

प्यार न सही
पर फिक्र करते हैं
दुआओं में ही सही
पर जिक्र करते हैं
अपना न सही
पर तेरा ख्याल करते हैं
तू रहे सलामत
बस यही फरियाद करते हैं
हम हर रोज मुस्कुराते है
फिर भी तेरे चेहरे का
मुस्कान हम याद करते हैं
प्यार न सही
पर फिक्र करते हैं
दुआओं में ही सही
पर जिक्र करते हैं

KRISHAN KANT SEN

इंतजार

एक एहसास है ज़िन्दगी, हसरतों से भरी हुई।
अनकहे से अल्फाज़ है,कुछ कहानी सुनी हुई।

उसकी यादों में मैं गुम हूँ या वो मुझमें कहीं गुम है।
पल पल घुटती चिन्ता में, मेरा गम भी क्या कम है।

बैठा करते थे झूले पर,अब चाय की चुस्कियाँ नम है।
दूर कहीं खो गया वो, घाव पर नही लगता मरहम है।

तन्हाइयों में खो गये, छंदो की लिपि के उलझे से स्वर।
बिन तुम्हे देखे खिलखिलाते, बढ़ता ही रहा मेरा ज्वर।

दो जिस्म और जान एक थे, बिखरे बिखरे लगते हो।
क्या कसक है तुम्हारे मन में,वाणी में भी लरजते हो।

कहाँ खो गया वो प्यार, कतरा कतरा आँसू बहते हैं।
लौट आओ अब तो यार, तुम बिन पल पल मरते हैं।

आँखों से नितझलकती उदासी,दूर तुमसे कब करती है।
पुकारो तो इक दफ़ा मन से, बस यही इंतजार करती है।

MANSHA PODDAR

A Special Gift

Today isn't a simple day,
It's a day of her birth.
Things that she never thought of,
She found it worth.

Day by Day her love grew strong,
She corrected me whenever I was wrong.
Time changed and so did the season,
To love her more she was the only reason.

Her every talk, her every giggle.
Made my heart restless as it starts to wriggle.
Her every talk and her every smile.
Made every moment of mine a worthwhile.

As I long last for her kiss,
Every moment the more I miss.
Her cute little face reveals her obedient soul.
Even if she wants to be naughty she can't reach the pole.

My baby turns ten, my head shall rejoice,
She was my last and I was her first choice.
I claim her my everything I love for sure,
As I change my calendar I will love her a little more.

First Call Her Brave...

Don't call her pretty first,
Call her brave and strong.
For all those fights she won herself,
For all those times her soul was crushed,
But still she chose to stay strong,
For all the love she gave to her loved ones without a question,
For all the dreams she is trying to fulfill,
For all the hatred she turned to love,
Yes, she is pretty but call her brave first!

She is a source of energy,
How can you deprive her?
Your existence came because of her periods,
How can you torture her?
She suffers tremendous pain for you,
To sund an awful abuse?
She converted her life into your life,
Please you only don't make her cry,
Yes, she is pretty but call her brave first!

Before watching her dress,
First watch your eyes,
Before watching her weakness,
First watch her strength,
Before buying for alchohol,
First buy her sanitary pads,
Befor respecting her in front of the crowd,
First respect her in front of yourself,
Yes, she is pretty but call her brave first!

SUMIT NASEEM

Rain

Inside me is a volcano outside it is just the rain..
The crazy memories of yours sometimes drive me insane..
I do not know why you started this dillusional chain..
The thing is no one got anything to gain...
All i wish to say is i want to just sleep in your brain.....

V. RATHIKA

Our Unconditional Love

Enchanting life I live with you
"Fairy tale," says most of the people
But our unconditional love for each other
Brought us together
In times of despair.
Destiny brought us together
In spite of rejection and hatred for each other
But love bloomed between us
Slowly, after we got to know each other.
Days were miserable for us,
An invisible line separated us marking our differences
We struggled to erase the line between us
But in the end when we met halfway through
Realising our love for each other
The invincible line vanished forever
We made the impossible possible!
Leaving the rest of the world in awestruck.
I am not sure whether I am the princess
For the rest of the nation
But I am the Queen of your noble heart!
You are the great strength for me,
My heart was pained
Seeing you with your previous love
But I was wrong
In the end, you showed me
 I am your heartbeat
And what is true love!
We are two separate persons
With one racing heart
I love the way you be,

I love it when you smile.
I love this world
When you are by my side
O! This is the end of "Princess Hour",
So be it!

PRAGYA VERMA

Our Hearts Never Let Us Separate

Our hearts never let us separate,
Due to this, we both just can't hate.
Our love is enough for both of us,
This makes our relationship flawless.

We see our beautiful future together,
Hoping always best for each other.
Standing together in every situation,
Our relationship has no complications.

Together we roam every place.
And create memories to embrace.
Shower our love on each other,
We are the better half of each other.

Staying together for so many years,
And counting more and more years.
This love story needs more happiness,
To get the taste of love and its loveliness.

JEEVITHA.S

Love - A Complete Invocation !

Love is something that makes you realize your worth,
 Love is something that never makes you feel down,
 Love is something that makes you wonder how crazy you are ;
Love is something that makes you believe in things ,
Love is something that makes you feel comfortable in the way you are!
Love is something which makes you to feel every little things ,
Love is something which could show you that ,
The whole world of yours could be a single person .
Love exists in that one person who means the world to you !

Love Is Like A Rain

It is very pleasing while drizzling and there comes the misunderstandings as lightening and fights as thunder making the love rain pour more even though it freaks us out for a while. Do we hate rain because of thunder and lightening ? Nah. I guess it won't rain without them if it does too the rain won't last longer and won't that be beautiful if it rains with that happiness sun on, making the life sky alluring.

NOMITA BAIDYA

सुभ नोमी

दुनिया की नज़रों में दो थे, लेकिन सुभ के नज़रों में सिर्फ नोमी थी और नोमी के नज़रों सिर्फ सूभ थे, प्रेम सिर्फ पाने का नाम नहीं ना ही प्रेम न मिलने से खो जाता है सच्चा प्रेम अनमोल होता हैं। प्रेम में शब्दों का खेल नहीं होता है। यहां तो आंखो से सब बया कर दिया जाता हैं। सच्चे प्रेम में तो उनकी यादें में छू जाये तो पता चल जता है की वो आपकी याद कर रहे है ।।

प्रेम से बोर कर कुछ नहीं हैं

संसार में प्रेम ही सब कुछ हैं

# ANUPAMA BAIDYA

Love

The most wonderful of all things in life , I believe , is the discovery of another human being with whom one's relationship has a glowing depth beauty and joy as the years increase. This inner progressiveness of love between two human beings is a most marvellous thing in cannot be found by looking for it or by passionately wishing it . It is a sort of divine accident .

AMAN SHARMA

Everlasting Love, Two Hearts One Life.

After all this time,
I thought it was just my heart that hurt
and could have broken into two,
but today I felt something
deeper beside my heart
and my lungs...
I think maybe it was my soul
or may it was my bonebreak...
It started as a dull ache in my ribs
and tightened my lungs
so my heart, my breaths
became short and then,
then I felt
her heart beside mine.

KONKI KAMAL SHARON

A Woman Love

Something hits me so hard, how a person can love the other with an extremely intense towards her. May be they treats the one who love as a blessing or may be there is a chance where they gets connected with the heart. Love for the other person is like a seed which turned into a plant. For the growth of the tree we used to water it daily. The only thing which keeps a tree growing is the essence of water. Here the same thing is in love. When we fall in love we don't know what a soul needs from us. Usually when I see the people and their love towards the other person makes me feel like really this thing Exists? May be Yes. The love I am going to talk about is not about the love of opposite sex. But here I wanted to give a little gesture about the love of a Girl who gets married and leave their Parents. I can say if you want to prove the love is greatest of all the only existing proof is Women. She survives more than anything else.

When a woman step out from mother house Just to bright the faces of her mother-in-law house is a love which she was bought up. Without women's love there is nothing more like colourful life. She spreads the Joy and Sparkle of Happiness in both the houses. Without her Presence house will not look like a blessed one. If you're loved by your mother, sister, a female friend, wife. You are the luckiest Person if you are nurtured by a Woman. Her Sparkle will help you even you are very from her.

Don't worry about the negative aspects in your life. If a stone hits you hard, crack it into pieces. Love is a thread that stables every unstable things. Respect a woman the most far she is the most close to heart.

RUBLEENA BEHERA

∆ वो वक्त नहीं इंतजार का जो तुम्हारे लिए गुजारी हुं।
तन्हाइयों की सड़कों पर कभी खुद को उतारी हूं।
तुम ही हो मंजिल मेरी और जिने का साहारा हो।
नसै की क्या जरूरत, नसा तुम्हारा सबसे प्यारा है।
तुम्हारे ही इश्क़ ने तो हमें रोज़ सवारा है,
वो वक्त नहीं इंतजार का जो तुम्हारे बिन गुजरी हूं ।

∆जो बुरे वक्त को अच्छे में बदल सकते हैं।
दौर भी उन्हीं का आता है।
और शायरी लिखना सिर्फ लफ़्ज़ों का खेल नहीं, जनाब!
कब? कैसे? क्या? क्यों लिखना है?
यह वक्त ही सिखाता है।

UPDESH CARPENTER

1) में इतना तोह नही जानता
की क्या तू हे बेवफ़ा या फिर तेरी कोई मजबूरी है
मगर में इतना तोह जान गया
की मेरे हाथों में तेरे नाम की लकीरें अधूरी है

2) बिन हवा तो ये पत्ते भी नही उड़ते
बिन मोड़ तो ये रास्ते भी नही मुड़ते
आखिर कोई तो वजह होगी उनके यूह बिन बताये चले जाने की
बिन कोई बात तो ऐसे रिश्ते नही तुड़ते

3) जीते जी टूट गया हूं
हाँ में उससे रूठ गया हूं
क्योकि उसे तोह न खयाल है न फिक्र मेरी
देखा तक नही की में पीछे छूट गया हूं

4) दिन रात देखे सिर्फ तेरे ही ख्वाब
तेरे पीछे सारी जिंदगी गवा दी
मगर आखिर में हम जुदा हो ही गये
न जाने खुदा ने ये किस जन्म की सज़ा दी

ASHISH KUMAR PATHAK

The pain of emotions
Love was my strength
When it was my mother
Whom I loved the most,
Love was my pleasure
When it was my friends
Who made me smile
Even in the toughest situations
Love was my peace
When it was with books
And my personal hobbies
But All of a sudden
Love became my weakness
When it happened
With someone unknown
She was beautiful but cunning
She played with my emotions
She made me weak and desperate
I began to trust her more
Than myself which was strange
I cared for her
More than I cared for myself as well
I became blind and deaf in her love
Her smile made my day
Her hug made me feel alive
Her happiness became my objective
And her company became my desire
If she cried, my heart wept with her
If she smiled, my heart jumped with joy
But she left me alone
Broken, lost and shattered
Now I understand it was not love
Love can not be one's weakness
And if it does, then it is not love.

RIYA VISHNOI

Soul

Every time tried to confess and fly
Hold to plead something arise
Whenever begin never finished
Swallow those words
because of fear of worst
Painful desire dreamy aspire
Taken back slowly
Those feelings of unsaid.

MONALISHA PANDA

Everlasting Love Two Hearts One Life

Few years ago. There was a little village named Shampur in the city . In this village all peoples were living together and every people help each other in their difficult times or bad times . In this village a handsome well behaved boy lived. His name was Kabir . He was 20 years old and his character was so good . Also he was a brilliant student in his village . Also in this village has a pretty beautiful girl lived . Her name was Priti . Priti was decent girl and her behaved was so humble . She respected all her elders and affectionated to all her youngers . She also kind hearted girl . Kabir and Priti both were studying at one clg and one stream . Also they were good for each other. They sat and discussion their study . In this way they also loved each other . Everyone feeled jealous for them and their love . one of them tried to break their love and finally they unsuccessful their plan . Their love bonding can't break his false word . They loved each other purely and their faith for each other was top most . May be they have two heart , two body but their life changed into one life . Their's love proved that "Love can be changed two hearts into one life ". Hence , spoken love can be changed into one life and also fulfilled a dream that seen by two people .

KRISHNA KANTHI TILAK G

The Rhythm Of Two Entangled Hearts

These two hearts ever knew that it would be tightly entwined so easily. Sakruti who met Sunil, on a chat site, didn't expect their lives that were completely different, would bring them so close and make their hearts stay connected to each others.

Sunil, who stayed in Delhi and Sakruti who resided in Bangalore, were far flung from each other, and couldn't resist their chatting regularly. They both were working, but still made their time to spent in each other's company. They spent chatting for hours together where time was even envy of them. And they ever got an idea about seeing each other either by photos or through video calls.

One fine morning, Sakruti couldn't stop her heart from asking a picture of his, so that, she could figure out about Sunil, was true, the way she imagined?! And without any delay, Sunil shared his photos. Sakruti, to her beautiful surprise, couldn't believe that he's the same, where she all the time dreamt off!! And same happened with Sunil, when she shared the pictures of hers. They felt, as if their bond was lingering from many years...

Each day they spent, made them feel special, with the sparkle in their eyes, with the heebie-jeebies in their frames, and moreover the feelings they had in their hearts for each other was with the same tune and the rhythm keeping their hearts close by. Their chat eventually turned out into making video calls, where they first saw one-on-one, and literally were on cloud nine, flying amidst the cooling clouds, soothing breeze and flocks of birds.

They could realize that there's a long way for them to travel in their journey of love, and also they could discern that they would face the tussle in the coming years ahead, as they were

entirely diverse. Love, along with their streak of hope kept the hearts charging continually that, though they were out of the way, their physical frames too in a distance, their hearts was one that was blossoming forever in the garden of love. "TRUE LOVE NEVER FADES OUT, INSTEAD KEEPS THE PERSONS HEART BLOOMING TOGETHER, FOREVER!!"

ANIRUDDHA DEEPAK GOHIL

Feeling Which Never Ends Irrespective Of Any Relations

Mother-Son, Father-Daughter, or Mother-Daughter. All these relations have natural unconditional love which in turn always tries to give, rather than taking or exchanging. But, eternal love is a feeling which never ends irrespective of any relations, or bonds. It is about instilling trust in the one we love with the feeling and expression that I will be always there for you without expecting anything.

Is it possible? YES! You can even love someone without staying with them and wishing well for them. It is also about your ability to love that special one. It is a journey without any destination. Though, you can have many milestones :)

It is all about being loved or to love that lasts forever!

DEBAPRIYO ROUT

Blended Emotions

It was the month of October, when the temperature is sometimes like that in the North Poles. Being a backbencher has its own advantages and disadvantages, the cold soothing breeze entered through the window and touched my rough skin making it dry. Trying to make my skin wet, i sprinkled some water on my face. I was then reading a novel, when the crackling sound of wrappers caught my attention. "Happy Birthday". "Thank you". There it was the disadvantage. I can here a voice of a girl but couldn't see her face, only thing I could see was big black heads in front of me. It was like a miracle when a boy bent down to pick up his pencil. The face was now clear. An oval shaped face with chubby Cheeks, brown eyes with kajal border, and a smile of heaven, who can ignore this face. Perfect! I wondered. With her distributing chocolates to my classmates, and me looking at her with eyes full of love made a filmy atmosphere, and everything else appeared still. But it can only happen in dream world It was then when She was walking towards the last bench. Sitting alone in a bench gave me Goosebumps. Even the stage didn't make me nervous. The moment created was like that the distance between us was indirectly proportional to my heartbeat. "Excuse me ? You there", she said holding the chocolate. Fuck did she hear me!
"Yes I am here always."
"What."
"No, that's not what I meant, I mean I did say that but not in other way. Ugh! Sorry, Happy Birthday."
Everyone looked at me with an opened mouth as if they saw a ghost. It was like God had made this one for me. She sat beside me, on the Bench next to me.
Perfect! Just Perfect

MEENAKSHI

प्रेम बंधन नहीं ,
प्रेम आजादी हैं
प्रेम दो जिस्मो का मिलन नहीं ,
प्रेम दो आत्माओं का मिलन है

प्रेम धोखा नहीं ,
प्रेम विश्वास हैं
प्रेम क्रोध नहीं,
प्रेम, प्रेम हैं

प्रेम जिस्म नहीं ,
प्रेम रूह हैं
प्रेम अपमान नहीं,
प्रेम सम्मान हैं

प्रेम अभिशाप नहीं,
प्रेम वरदान हैं
प्रेम कुरूप नहीं ,
प्रेम सुंदर हैं

प्रेम चेहरे की सुंदरता नहीं ,
प्रेम हृदय की सुंदरता हैं
प्रेम तीखा तो,
प्रेम मिठास भी हैं

प्रेम सुंदर ही नहीं,
प्रेम का हर नजरिया ही सुन्दर हैं
प्रेम में सब कुछ पाना ही नहीं ,
प्रेम में कभी - कभी बहुत कुछ खोना भी होता हैं।..

SHIVANJALI SRIVASTAVA

Sublime Love

Do you know what is love? ..... Everyone would say; romantic conversation, dating, calling with sweet nicknames is love. Actually no, love is not only about romantic conversation, dating, candle light dinner, or cuddling with each other.

 Love is a beautiful flower, which when bloom in someone's heart, it fumes his/her soul with extreme pleasure and the person get lost itself in world of imagination. Love is also another name of sacrifice which should be seen from both the sides, some compromise and some true promises which last forever.

Have you ever heard about Sublime love?

It's kind of everlasting love, which connects two different hearts into single beautiful soul. In other words, we can say that Sublime love is nothing else but is what true love.

True love is a segmentation of affection, care, mutual understanding, some fights, apologies, some sorrows and sharing of happiness between two pure souls, a beautiful connection of two minds, flow of attraction towards each other hearts. It is unconditional and always remaining loyal for each other. True love can be said, when you respect each other's dissimilarities and accepting the way other one is.

I would like to conclude it with a feeling or emotion what one feel when he/she is into someone: " You are my heart, my life, my one and only thought. My world is into you. Your arms are my rest zone, my comfort zone. Your company gives me a kind of strength, my life gets complete with you."

MAHITIXA TANK

शाश्वत

जिस्म की क्या जरूरत करे,
इसकी क्या हिफाजत करे;
आपने रूह को सुकून दिया,
अब खुदा से क्या सजदे करे।

धड़कन की क्या रिहायत करे;
इसकी क्या किफायत करे;
आपने 'अविनाश' धड़का लिया,
अब ख़ुद को क्या इनायत करें?

हमारी प्रीत शाश्वत है,
अब हर जनम क्या एतबार करे!?

SHIVANGI SRIVASTAVA

"Pure Love"

Since now you are here,
I feel the love so dear.
Its you, to whom I actually belong,
And so the feeling is very strong.
The only one who can make me laugh while I want to cry,
And make me live while I want to die.
Whenever in my life, there is a dark night,
Its in your eyes where I find my bright light.
With your just one look, I begin to blush,
I just want to tell you that I love you so much.
My love is eternal and will withstand every pain,
For it is so pure that it expects no gain.
This is my purest love confession,
Since you are my most precious possession.

JHUNU SWAIN

LOVE

Love is the purity
Love is the glory
Love is the sweetness
Love is the divinity
And love also is the fascinatiny

Love give us sympathy
Love give us dignity
And love also gives us sincerity
Love can healings our all pain
Love can do every incredible things
And love also can pray for us

Brightness blessing, attachment
All where staying love
Love love love
Every heart needs love

One day
One day everything will be finished,
and, nothing will be
In this world
False is nothing and
False is everything, so

This world just has full of mystery
And, everything looks glittering
But that not the gold
And every thing has deep meaning
Because of all are god created things

In our life
One day everything will be finished, and
Nothing will be
Just only the end of life.

ROMY KUMAR

Adhuri Khawish
jism apna tum kisi aur ko dee aana,
Mere liye apni tum bs ruh le aana !

Ussi main guzaar denge keyin sadiyaan,
Tum rab se zindagi ki mohollat le aana !

Kitni baar dil churaya hai usne mera,
Aate aate tum apna jumka sath le aana !

Uske noor ke aage sb feeke pd jayengye,
Aee duniawalo, tum chaandh sitare sb le aana !

Apni bewafayi main sari kaynaat main manta hun,
Tum bs muje 2 -4 swalat ka mouka de jaana !

Le aana ikk phool meri kabr par,
Meri adhuri mout ko tum mukammal bna jana !

AJAY BORASI

मोहब्बत क्या है,

समझो तो एहसास,

देखो तो रिश्ता, कहो तो लफ़्ज,

चाहो तो जिंदगी,

करो तो इबादत ,   निभाओ तो वादा,

और मिल जाए तो जन्नत है   जो व्यक्ति दूर होते हुए भी

हमारे आस-पास लगे..

तो ..समझ लेना ..उस व्यक्ति से आपको मोहब्बत हो गई है   बंधनों

में बाँधना, मोहब्बत नहीं...

खुला आसमान दे देना, मोहब्बत है...जो आपका गुस्सा सहन

करके भी आपका साथ दे,

आपसे बातें करें उससे ज्यादा मोहब्बत आपको

कोई नहीं कर सकता जब मोहब्बत तन से नही मन से

होता है, तो इंतज़ार भी

बेशुमार होता है, और प्यार भी

बेशुमार होता है मोहब्बत तो अनपढ़ ही होती है,साहेब

किसी को देखा है मोहब्बत में डिग्री लेते हुए

ZAINAB SABOOWALA

Love Is Bliss

Love happened
When your soul met mine
The eyes that says
I Love You every time
The warmth of your hug
When you hold me tight
You've got that smile
That makes my world shine
With you by my side
My happiness touches the sky
It's just you and everything else a lie
You're the one to rule my heart and mind
You are the song that my heart sings
Your presence in my life is a pure bliss
The moments with you are magical
My love for you is eternal.

ANWESHA MAHARANA

Everlasting Love, Two Hearts One Soul..

Morning I woke up,
Holding the pillow but he was mimicing you
Sun was just kissing me through the opening as if it was you.

Took me to that day,
pale sky,
In the crowdy soar, peoples' roar,
I could only hear your heartbeat murmer.

Moment is hard to express,
 in my blurry land of lenses.

Holding you tightly in the mess,
 bursting out my stress.
 I still remember your essence.

Tension had integrated,
love just arrived and got multiplied,
Powerfully, exponentially.

Time step away
wind of love caressing through my body,
I could only feel your coddling.

All the laws failed,
except the law of Love Opted.

RACHNA SANDIP MISTRY

Lifetime Of Love

One fine day I came across an elderly couple in garden. I sat at distance and observed them. They appeared to be in so much love with each other. The lady was sitting on one of the benches and was waiting for her husband. He came with a bouquet of red roses for her. They looked so happy. I was able to listen their conversation. She thanked him and told him, "you never forget our first meeting and on that day every year you gift me this bouquet of red roses without fail. I love you forever." Then he said, "the day I met you was such a precious and important day of my life that god gifted me with my soul mate who is always there with me in any type of situation. I can never stop thanking god for bringing you in my life and I pray to god to keep us together forever." By watching this I came to know that by care, trust and love any relation can last for a lifetime. I also wish I get my soul mate like them and our love lasts for a lifetime.

ANKITA DEB

How? It Remained Untold

I might never tell you,
The way you painted my heart with golden hue.
I was a trembling branch of an unhappy path,
You touched my soul which instantly mended me again which was once fallen apart.
Trampled under the burden of the sunken ship of ego,
You changed its route towards a dedicated vow!
I wasn't this before,
You translated my heart in your language and taught me to adore.
I was wandering in the dark fierce forest of sorrow,
You illuminated my entire path with aspiring fireflies which was nature's borrow,
I didn't discover the depth of miracles untill you were mine.
I can't even imagine the invisible thread of our fairy tale that's so fine.
I was a dumb who took your massive attention as relegation,
Oh! My pessimistic eyes fell for your optimistic soul as soon as you took it as reverence which was actually seclusion.
Your trauma and pain was beyond my imagination,
The nature blows the wind,which makes me to fly in your sky of compassion which always holds my passion above every tension.
Your script of love was untitled and unmatched with my dialect of heartly composition,
Reassuring my strings of heart you completed my love song with infinite direction.

YAMINI MANCHINENI

The Best Feelings

The Unknown Language Of Love Between Eyes Of Us!

The Wild Instinct Of Souls When We both Are Nearby!!

The Disturbing Adrenaline Rush When We Walked Towards Each Other!!!

"Find Your True One's To Experience This Sublime Love"

SITARA AKULA

Sublime Love

When two soul mate are meet,
then their
Eyes are saying
We will look after each other
Thoughts are saying
We will support each other
Hands are saying
We will protect each other
And Each Heart is saying
I m there for you

Our love like a sky
Disturbances like clouds
affection like rains
Quarrels like heat
Appraisals like stars
Our relationship graph like
Sun rises and sets
So it is everlasting

We are
Two containers
Two hearts
But one soul

Evidencing their love with exchange of rings be like

One heart beat is saying
To another heart beat
I am there for you now

We are going to be one heart beat

 Meaning of events

Before engagement
Finding a soulmate

At engagement
Evidencing love with exchange of rings

At wedding
We are going to become one heartbeat

After wedding
We are becoming one person

MANOJ SONDHIYA

इश्कबाज़ी

हुई थीं जब मुलाकात उनसे मुझमें जोश भरा सा था,
कब हो गई मोहब्ब्त उनसे हमे जरा भी होश ना था...

चंद बातो में उनसे हमारी मानो जैसे दोस्ती पुरानी हो गई,
ना जाने उसे खुद पता नहीं चला और मेरी दीवानी हो गई...

मिलने जुलने का सिलसिला इस तरह शुरू हुआ हमारा,
दिल में ही दोनों ने एक दुजे को सौंप दिया अपना संसार सारा...

कभी कभी होती थी छुप छुप कर प्यार भरी मुलाकाते,
तो कभी एक दूसरे की यादो में ही बीत जाती थी राते..

जब तक दिदार ना हो जाये उनका गले के नीचे निवाला नही जाता
था,
उनकी आवाज को तरस जाये जब तक फ़ोन नही आता था...

है ये इश्क बड़ा ही बदनाम जिसने भी इसे बनाया है,
लेकिन नाम उसका भी गुमनाम जिसने आखिरी सांस तक निभाया
है...

PRASAD BABU GALLA

Undefined Sublime

Undefined sublime love
Of my heart calling
for My body senses
to touch your sweet lips.

My lips eagerly
waiting for your kiss.

Undefined sublime love
Of my heart calling
for embracing love
of unknown desires.

I want to die in your arms
with embracing eternal love.

SANJEET KUMAR

प्रेम और परिंदे!

नादान थे हम वो परिंदो कि तरह उड़ गए।
हम गम में क्या डूबे वो लाखो पे मरने लगे।

जिस तरह वादे किए थे नम आंखों से जुदा भी हो गए।
नादान थे हम वो परिंदो कि तरह उड़ गए।

पत्थर दिल थे वो जो हमे भूल गए।
नादान थे हम वो परिंदो कि तरह उड़ गए।

हम प्रेम की नईया चलाने वाले थे वो दुवाओ में बस गए
नादान थे हम वो परिंदो कि तरह उड़ गए।

सोचा था बन जाऊंगा मैं सफर पर वो किसी और के हम- सफर हो गए।
नादान थे हम वो परिंदो कि तरह उड़ गए।

लालच थी बस एक प्रेम की, और झुक के हम टूट गए।
नादान थे हम वो परिंदो कि तरह उड़ गए।

NAINA DEKA

Hazy Dawn

Ding...Dong...

Rajat came downstairs, hearing the doorbell ring the second time.

"What Kamla Bai? Late again? Radhika is not going to spare you this time."

He let her in with a razzing smile.

Kamla Bai just gazed at him blankly.

"Come on. What are you waiting for? Get to work fast. I have lots of preparations left for tomorrow."

Rajat started packing his office bag and continued to speak.

"Tomorrow is Radhika's birthday. It is her first birthday after our marriage and I am planning to throw a grand party. However, it should be a surprise for her. Don't you dare to tell her anything okay?"

Rajat gave an interrogative look to Kamla Bai.

To that, she made a gesture by moving her hands in a particular way, with the same blank look.

Suddenly he realised how stupid of him it was, to ask such a question knowing the fact that she could not speak.

Rajat clearly remembered the day he brought her home nine months back, just after his marriage with Radhika. Both of them being busy with their jobs the whole day, they required someone to look after the house and Kamla Bai was the most compatible one.

"After doing the dishes you can directly start cleaning the house. Don't worry about the breakfast. I have prepared everything of Radhika's choice. Now let me go upstairs and check. This girl is getting lazier day by day."

Kamla Bai kept on staring at the stairs until Rajat disappeared into his room.

"Get up my love. How can you sleep for so long? Let's do breakfast together. I have prepared everything that you like."
Rajat sat down on the bed beside her, gently running his fingers over her supple hair. Radhika kept on lying down with her eyes closed surrounded by all the monitoring equipments required to support a comatose patient.
"I have been waking you up since the last six months and you don't even respond. How can someone be so stubborn Radhika?"
That incident still haunted Rajat. It was just three months after their marriage, when Radhika was on her way to the airport to receive him. He was dying to see her face after an official tour of seven long days. Nevertheless, what he was unaware of was the destiny. That one accident snatched away all his happiness. The doctors announced that she went into coma for an indefinite period. But Rajat would just not give up.
Knock...Knock...
"Come in Kamla Bai. It seems Madam is not in a mood to get up today."
He gave a faint smile and left the room.
Kamla Bai looked at Radhika and let out a sigh.

The End

That Girl

It's the story of a girl
Who no more dances in the rain.

The brightest light in the chandeliar
The prettiest flower in the garden,
The true belle on the dance floor
It's about her pain.

It's about a girl
Who no more dances in the rain.

The sky seems too far to reach
But she's not afraid,
Coz the stars belong to her
And that's all she wants to gain.

It's about a girl
Who no more dances in the rain.

The smell of the seasons whirl around
The tune of those old memories whisper,
The mirror longs for that lovely old smile
Will she be truly happy again?

It's about a girl
Who no more dances in the rain.

AMAN AGRAWAL

जब जब वो गुस्से से अपना मुंह फुलाती है ,

कसम मेरी जान की मेरी आधी जान तो यूं ही चली जाती है ,

ख्वाबों की मलिका कहूं उसे या केह दूं मेरे दिल की शहजादी ,

जबसे आई वो मेरी ज़िन्दगी में हुई है हर तरफ ही ज़िन्दगी में आबादी,

जिस्म उसका दिल उसका ज़र्रे ज़र्रे में अब वो है ,

जिक्र उसका फिक्र उसकी कतरे कतरे में अब वो है ...

दिल तो दे ही बैठे है सनम आपको हम,

जान अब आप पर लुटाने का वादा है ,

कैसे कहूं क्या है अब आरज़ू इस दिल की ...

बस साथ जीने के बाद अकेले मर जाने का इरादा है ...

सवाल था मर कर भी उठ खड़े होने का..

तेरा हाथ तेरा साथ ही इसमें मेरे काम आया ...

जब जब हुई महफ़िल में इश्क़ की सीरत की बात ,

कसम से मेरी जान मेरे लबों पे सिर्फ तेरा ही अब नाम आया ...

तू ज़िन्दगी तू दुआ तू ही तो अब मेरी जान है ...

मेरी ज़िन्दगी भर की गई खामोश सी मोहब्बत का अब तू ही तो एक ईनाम है ...

तू जो मिली सब मिल गया .. ज़िन्दगी में अब खुशियों वाला फूल खिल गया ..

PUJA BAGARTI

Everlasting Love Two Heart One Life_

When colours of your love paint in my life.......
My life change into a beautiful life.
OH MY BELOVED,
First this heart beat for mine...
But now,
It's beat for want to see you with mine.....
When the cloud start thundering,
Then the feeling of a peacock,
That's like my heart feel when I see you..
You.....
You are like the star in my life....
Your shining light give shine in my life.
You my love you........
You are the reason why I love dreaming....
Because that was the one and only place where I live with you permanently....
My love.....
My heartbeat beats faster when someone told your name Infront of mine...
And, listen my dear,
I don't need any expensive things in my life....
Cause for me you are my expensive.
Don't know what God want with us....
But no Matter what happens in my life you always still in my heart as a special place as a special person....
EVERYONE HAVE A SPIRIT,
BUT, WHEN TWO SPIRIT CAME CLOSER AND THEY LIVE FOR EACHOTHER,
THEN THEY WERE CALLED TWO HEART ONE LIFE.

RAJESH KUMAR SAHOO

Love Vs Curse

What happened everywhere?
Humans are suffering except nature;
Pandemic is the only reality everywhere,
"Save us" "Save us" is the only prayer.

A small invisible virus makes us realise;
How much a life is precious;
No status, no bank balance,no ego
Except nature no one can save us .

Mother nature's Love is always eternal,
We didn't realise it and spoiled everything,
Now the return is in form of deadly virus,
It's final a reminder to rectify everything.

Love Defines

Love is a beautiful language,
In which Love is the word,
In which Love is the feeling,
In which Love makes every word live.

Love is the beautiful derivative of Trust and Loyalty,
Love is a beautiful equation of two souls,
Love is a powerful motivator during storm,
Love is the only truth and rest all false.

"Tears or smile" Love is in both.
That's why a tear drop seems much heavier,
And smile becomes everything for us.
This is how the "Love" defines life easier.

Beautiful All About

I saw a small kid with a paper boat,
He was about to sail it on rain water,
For the world the incident may be a child ish one,
"Childhood is really beautiful."

I saw a old aged couple were eating ice cream at park,
Their cute expressions for each other was awesome,
They were caring each other like one soul,
This "Love is beautiful"

I saw a mother was looking for her son at an old age home,
Even after her son has left her for old age,
Still mother is looking for when her son will come to meet her,
This "Love is eternal and beautiful"

SANDHIYA. S

You

I never asked for your love
I never asked for your attention
All I've been asked is your smile and happiness

The way you laugh
The way you talk
The way you walk
Always heal my pain

You're like a sweet medicine
That I always take even when I'm not sick
You're like a soft sweater
That always makes me feel warm even when I'm not cold
You're like the air
And without you, I can't breathe

I never say that I love you
Or that I adore you
But I hope you feel my love to you

And I also hope
The reason you laugh like that
You talk like that
You walk like that
Is me

SHOWMEN TALUKDAR

Love is the most pure feeling in the world.
But in recent times we see people are afraid to love again after a terrible breakup or past..We all want our love to be everlasting love but for most of us it is not in our fate or I should say destiny..
Life is unpredictable as well sometimes we fall in love with a person who is not with us and sometimes it happens that both of them wants to be together but destiny just turns apart...
We cannot term it as it wasn't love..
But the time wasn't the right time for love..
It happens not only in stories or cinemas but also in real life that the person we love comes back after a certain time...
And that's the time where everything falls in its place..
When the universe also tried to bend itself in front of the love of their beloved.
That's when the saying for anyone who love comes true
"Love is everlasting when two hearts becomes one soul".

SPARSH KULSHRETHA

Achha lagta hai
Tum se baatein karna
Achha lagta hai
Tumhari taarifein karna
Achha lagta hai
Kit um ho saath mere
Achha lagta hai
Kit um dil ko samajhti ho
Achha lagta hai
Tumhara aakhe jhukana
Achha lagta hai
Tumhara bin baat rooth jan
Achha lagta hai
Din k kuch pal tumhare
Saath bitana
Achha lagta hai
Tumhare bare me likhne jana
Achha lagta hai
Mere dil ko tumhari yaadon
Mein kho jana.

Flairs and Glairs, a platform by a student for the students. We are esteemed youth struggling to carve out our path for our future and we follow a basic mindset Since everyone is not born with all-round skills. Joining hands with people who are born to execute it with perfection is the best way to evolve. Self-Evolution is the need of the hour but, evolving as a community is what we strive for. The initiative as kickstarted by, Founder- Mr. Shubham Shah with the motive to utilize the skillset and talent of writing has now a team of 10+ people who are actively participating into newer forms of learning and discovering talents among youngsters. We Provide platform and services like Publishing opportunities, Open mics, Workshops, Hands-on training. Operating with Brand Name of Flairs and Glairs (Publication House), we offer the chance of elevating a passionate writer to an esteemed author With Brand name Teekhe Zasbaaat. We bring to you an opportunity to get accustomed with the Public Speaking and Presenting of Thoughts along with regular challenges to brush up your inking spirit. The newest initiative to extend our services we introduced in a new writing Platform- The Glittering Fables and Ink Over Tears.

We Choose to Fly Like A Falcon than to be

a Leg Pulling Crab.

To Know More: Infoline – 7781900870
Mail Us At-
flairsandglairs@gmail.com / info@flairsandglairs.in
Or Visit is at
www.flairsandglairs.com / www.flairsandglairs.in
Social Handles- @flairsandglairs @teekhezasbaaat